D1476519

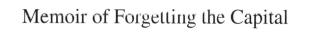

Memoir of Forgetting the Capital

Tanizaki Jun'ichirō 谷崎潤一郎 著

Memoir of Forgetting the Capital

Miyakowasure no ki 都わすれの記

Translated by

Amy V. Heinrich

Foreword by

Donald Keene

YUSHODO COMPANY LIMITED

Tokyo 2010

Memoir of Forgetting the Capital
Miyakowasure no ki by Tanizaki Jun'ichirō
English Translation by Amy V. Heinrich
Foreword by Donald Keene
originally published in the Japanese language
by Sogensha in 1948.

Copyright©2010
ISBN 978-4-8419-0547-2 (Japan)

All rights reserved.
No portion of this book may be reproduced,
by any process or technique,
without the express written consent of publisher.

Published by
Yushodo Co., Ltd.
27 Sakamachi, Shinjuku-ku,
Tokyo 160-0002 Japan

Printed by Mizuno Pritech Co., Ltd.

Distributed in U.S. by Columbia University Press
61 West 62nd Street New York,
New York 10023

Printed in Japan

PL
839
A7
S913
m
2010

Preface

In 1953, before I first went to Japan for study, the only living Japanese author whose name I knew or whose works I had read was Tanizaki Jun'ichirō. This must seem strange, considering I had already published several books about Japanese literature; but my interest was mainly in the classics rather than in modern literature. I had, however, received from the great translator Arthur Waley the copy of Tanizaki's *The Makioka Sisters* which Tanizaki had sent him, possibly in the hopes that Waley, the translator of *The Tale of Genji*, would translate his "Genji." I read *The Makioka Sisters* with admiration, and hoped I might meet the author while I was in Japan.

I was given a golden opportunity to meet Tanizaki by another eminent translator, Edward Seidensticker, who asked me to take to Tanizaki in Kyoto (where I then lived) the manuscript of his translation of *Some Prefer Nettles*. Seidensticker had a poor opinion of the Japanese postal system and thought I was more likely to deliver the manuscript safely.

I visited Tanizaki one warm late-summer day. The house was in a quiet part of Kyoto. As I waited for Tanizaki, I heard at regular intervals a sound like wooden blocks clapped together. Later I learned that this was a *shishi-odoshi*, or "deer frightener," a contrivance originally intended to scare away deer (or perhaps wild boars) when they were common in the hills surrounding the city. The sound lent a pleasantly rustic touch.

Tanizaki appeared soon afterwards. He wore a kimono, but not a *hakama*, which he said he disliked. He showed no hesitation in answering my questions about *The Makioka Sisters*. I asked if certain events described in the novel had actually occurred. A novelist is likely to reply to this question by insisting he had no one source and that the characters were amalgams of people he had known, but Tanizaki revealed that although there were elements of fiction, the events had been described more or less as they had occurred.

As I was about to leave, Tanizaki took two or three books from a shelf and gave them to me after first inscribing his name. One was *Miyakowasure no ki*. Although I was fairly well acquainted with Tanizaki's works, I had never heard of this book, I did not even realize that *miyakowasure* was the name of a flower, supposing it might be a term conveying nostalgia for the capital (*miyako*), a familiar theme in classical writing. When I got home, I opened the book and was surprised to discover it consisted mainly of poetry. I was not aware Tanizaki had written poetry.

I had almost forgotten about *Miyakowasure no ki* when Amy Heinrich mentioned that she was making a translation from my copy, which I had given to the Starr East Asian Library. Knowing of Amy's particular interest in tanka poetry—her doctoral dissertation was about the great tanka poet Saitō Mokichi, and she herself had composed tanka as a member of a group in Tokyo—I thought this would make for an excellent translation, and I was not mistaken. Amy's translation captures the tone of the original poems admirably. The sequence is a charming work that reveals a side to Tanizaki not found in his novels or plays, bringing the reader much closer to a man who many believe was the greatest Japanese writer of the twentieth century.

Donald Keene

Introduction

Tanizaki Jun'ichirō published the *tanka* sequence *Miyakowasure no ki* (*Memoir of Forgetting the Capital*) in 1953, about his experiences beginning in the spring of 1944, when he evacuated his home in the Osaka-Kobe region for fear of bombings.[1] He took along with him his daughter, his wife, and her two younger sisters. Together they moved first to Atami, then to Tsuyama, and later to Katsuyama, in Okayama prefecture, before finally returning to their burned-out home in the spring of 1946. Tanizaki was by then famous as a novelist—one of the giants of twentieth century fiction—and was in the midst of writing *Sasameyuki* (translated by Edward Seidensticker as *The Makioka Sisters*), apparently using the three sisters in his care, with the addition of the fourth sister not with them, as the models for the four sisters in the novel. He was also working on the second of his three modern translations of Murasaki Shikibu's *Genji monogatari* (*The Tale of Genji*).

The capital referred to in the name of the flower *miyakowasure* ("forgetting the capital") is the old capital of Kyoto, not Tokyo, the capital of Japan at the time. In the world of the poetic sequence, Tanizaki's use of "the capital" to mean Kyoto serves two purposes. First, it represents the Kansai region, where the Tanizakis made their home, the center of the world lost to them in their wartime wanderings. In addition, it places his poems squarely in the past when "the capital" did mean Kyoto, and so within the aura of the classical literary world which Tanizaki drew on in his poems. The language of both the poems and the head notes that introduce them in the sequence is classical Japanese, rather than modern, and the sequence begins by locating the poet and, especially, the women of the family, in a calm and elegant past.

The flower itself, the *miyakowasure*, is a wild spring aster that was not cultivated in Japan until the Edo period, and is not mentioned in classical poetry. It looks like a purple daisy, with a yellow center, and is rustic in appearance, more suited to a meadow than to a garden. But its name recalls the *miyakodori*, the "capital bird," famous from the following poem in the tenth-century *Ise monogatari* (*The Tales of Ise*),

---

1 Tanizaki Jun'ichirō. *Miyakowasure no ki* 『都わすれの記』 (*Memoir of Forgetting the Capital*), calligraphy by Tanizaki Matsuko, book design and illustration by Wada Sanzō. Osaka: Sogensha, 1948. A *tanka* ("short poem") is a thirty-one-syllable poem, usually called, in premodern times, a *waka* ("Japanese poem").

traditionally ascribed to Ariwara no Narihira, and often referred to throughout the ensuing centuries of Japanese poetry.

> **na ni shi owaba** *iza kototowamu miyakodori waga omou hito wa ari ya nashi ya to*
> > If you are faithful
> > To your name, I would ask you,
> > Bird of the city,
> > Is the woman I think of
> > Alive, or is she no more? [2]

The fourth poem under Section 4 refers directly to the Narihira poem, repeating its first line:

> **na ni shi owaba** *hana yo miyako wa wasuru tomo yo wo wabibito no ware na wasure so*
> > O blossoms! as you bear
> > it in your name, even as
> > you forget the capital,
> > do not forget those like me,
> > withdrawn from that world

The full sequence has seventy-two *tanka*, many with head notes; the poems are organized into 43 sections, and several of them include more than one poem—section 13 contains eight poems.[3] The entire text of the book—both head notes and poems—is written out by Tanizaki's wife Matsuko in elegantly beautiful calligraphy, and the book was designed and illustrated by Wada Sanzō.[4] (A printed pamphlet of the whole text is included with the hand-written volume, for legibility.) The volume as a whole provides a record of Tanizaki's experience of the two years from the spring of 1944, when the war was increasingly impinging on daily experience, through the defeat, the following fall and winter, and on to the spring of 1946. The references to the war are primarily in the head notes, rarely in the poems themselves. Section 12 mentions battles raging in the South Pacific. The head notes discuss such wartime

---

2   Translation by Donald Keene, in his *Seeds in the Heart: Japanese Literature from Earliest Times to the Late Sixteenth Century*. New York: Holt, Rinehart and Winston, 1993, p. 231.

3   The poems are 1, 2, 3, 4 (four poems), 5, 6, 7, 8, 9 (three poems), 10 (two poems), 11, 12, 13 (eight poems), 14, 15, 16, 17, 18 (two poems), 19, 20, 21, 22, 23, 24, 25 (three poems), 26, 27 (two poems), 28 (two poems), 29, 30 (three poems), 31, 32, 33 (two poems), 34, 35, 36, 37 (two poems), 38, 39 (four poems), 40, 41 (three poems), 42 (three poems), 43.

4   Wada Sanzō 和田三造 (1883-1967) was born in Hyōgo Prefecture; he studied Western art in Japan and Europe, and was particularly interested in color. Late in his life he produced prints that merged Western and Japanese styles.

issues as the reasons to evacuate specific areas; a young neighbor going to marry an official in China; an article in a newspaper about possible bombings; or the rumors of invasion. There is no political position overtly taken or assumed. The sequence presents an interesting human record, as the poems serve first to acknowledge and then to absorb changes, and in the end to contain and express the deep emotions brought about by those changes.

There are more allusions to the poetry classics in the early part of the sequence, chronologically earlier in the experience as a whole, as well as a playful use of classical poetic techniques. In the second poem, for example, mention of his actual departure from home, when his heart is going to stay on with the flowers in his garden, is in line four of the original poem, in the word *tatsu*, a pivot word (*kakekotoba*) whose meaning changes in relation to what precedes it, and what follows. The speaker of the poem (Section 2) is departing (one meaning of *tatsu*, here related to what comes before) as the mist is rising (the second meaning of *tatsu*, here related to the mist that follows, *kasumi*).

> *furusato no hana ni kokoro wo nokoshitsutsu* **tatsu** *ya kasumi no Ubara Sumiyoshi*
> > even as my heart remains
> > here with the flowers
> > of my old home,
> > > ah, how the mist is rising
> > > as I leave Sumiyoshi in Ubara

The next poem (Section 3) refers to an ancient poetic trope on how closely cherry blossom petals blown around by the wind resemble snow. There is nothing in the poems as they progress into the spring to indicate that the writer is living in modern times, during a brutal war. The poems create a world less frightening, more elegant, than the real one.

> *yamazato wa sakura fubuki ni akekurete hana naki niwa mo hana zo chirishiku*
> > day and night swirling
> > like blowing snow in this mountain
> > village, these cherry blossoms –
> > > even the garden without
> > > cherry trees   carpeted in blossoms

One of the first poems to reach deeper into emotions more raw than elegiac, Section 23, mentions the war directly only in the lengthy head note:

> *kakaru yo ni au koso ukere yoki toki ni waga chichi haha wa usetamaikeri*
>> o grief! to have lived
>> to meet a world such as this!
>> I lost them
>> in good time, my father
>>> and my mother

The poems apparently were indeed written chronologically, during the actual experience. But the head notes were not. In 1977, in time for the thirteenth anniversary of Tanizaki's death, his widow Matsuko privately published a large collection of his poems—mostly tanka but also some haiku.[5] The volume is printed on thick, cream-colored paper and beautifully bound in hand-woven fabric, in a limited edition of 150 copies. The poems in that volume have minimal head notes at most, presumably written at the time of each poem's composition. They are significantly expanded and changed when they appear with the versions of the poems Tanizaki published in *Miyakowasure no ki*. So the compilation encompasses both immediate responses and some hindsight description.

One of the first poems to lose entirely a sense of paying homage to the *waka* tradition is Section 26:

> *natsu no hi no atsuki megumi no hataketsumono emaku zo hoshiki mame mo tamana mo*
>> warmed and blessed
>> by the hot summer sun,
>> the fruit of the fields –
>> what we so longed for!
>> both the beans and the cabbage

Mention of the hot summer sun may have been possible, but there was no place in the poetic tradition for beans and cabbage. It is in the middle of the sequence that the tone begins to move toward a sparer poetic, one that has no time for literary games.

---

5 Tanizaki Jun'ichirō. *Tanizaki Jun'ichirō kashū*『谷崎潤一郎家集』. Osaka: Yukawa Shobō, 1977.

One of the last poems to allude to earlier poetry is Section 32, marking the end of the war:

*omoiyare **tsuwamono domo** ga tsurugi tachi suteshi yūbe no nobe no tsuyu kesa*
      only think of it!
      all the nation's warriors
      have discarded their
      long swords   last night's fields
                       heavy with dew, with tears

The words *tsuwamono domo* (the warriors) allude to a haiku by Matsuo Bashō (1644-1694), when he visited Hiraizumi, the site of the last stronghold of the Fujiwara clan. Their defeat marked the end of the Heian period in the late twelfth century.

*natsugusa ya **tsuwamono domo** ga yume no ato*
      The summer grasses –
      For many brave warriors
      The aftermath of dreams[6]

To Bashō, those warriors had been dead for five hundred years. To Tanizaki, Bashō himself was two hundred and fifty years gone. By placing Japan's defeat in 1945 in a context of nearly eight hundred years of deaths in battle, Tanizaki is seeing a universal sorrow, an enduring human futility, in the waging of war.

By this time in the seventy-two-poem sequence, Tanizaki has mostly moved away from poetic allusion and focused on the ordinary in life, sparrows rather than *miyakodori* (capital birds), albeit doing extraordinary things (Section 28):

mado no to wo akureba iriku yamazato no hito ni naretaru suzume uguisu
      when I open the shutters
      in they come –
            accustomed to people
            in the mountain village,
            the swallow, the warbler

---

6   The translation is by Donald Keene, in his *World within Walls: Japanese Literature of the Pre-Modern Era, 1600-1867*. New York: Holt, Rinehart and Winston, 1976, p. 104.

The months after the war ended are the hardest for Tanizaki and his family: commodities were scarce, food was hard to come by, and the future was uncertain. The winter was a long and weary one in Section 37, Poem 2:

> *susamaji to kanete mo kikishi yamazato no mono mina ko'oru fuyu wa kinikeri*
> I've already heard
> how dreadful it is – winter,
> when everything
> in this mountain village
> freezes – winter has come

The weight of the snow is considerable—on eaves, covering mountains, leaving behind icicles. Spring becomes less a glorious bursting forth than an apparent contradiction; it is certainly a striking contrast with the sober reality around it, far removed from the trailing sleeves of the ladies viewing cherry blossoms, or the bevy of sisters who surpassed the splendor of spring in his memory earlier in the sequence. In Section 42, Poem 3, the context of defeat and how altered the people were by the wartime experience takes precedence.

> *kuni wa yabure hito wa susamishi haru nagara miyako wa Saga no hana zakari kana*
> the nation defeated,
> the people grown rough –
>   even so it is spring –
> the capital, with
> Saga in full bloom

So while spring is hope, for growth and beauty, and for recovery, there are no images of plum blossoms or cherry blossoms; spring is instead the absence of winter. The scars of the wartime experience are undeniable. But the love in the final poem, no longer idealized and elegant but physical and poignant, seems stronger.

> *asanegami makite medenishi ikutose no tanare no kao mo yasenikerashi na*
> stroking your
> tousled hair, beloved,
>   for so many years
>   familiar to my touch,
> how thin your face has grown

From the literary playfulness of the earliest poems, Tanizaki's poems seem to have grown into a deeply observant record of changing emotion, markers on the way to ordering his experiences over a turbulent time.

Amy V. Heinrich

I am deeply grateful to Donald Keene for introducing me to the volume *Miyakowasure no ki*, which he received from Tanizaki in 1953, and donated to the C. V. Starr East Asian Library; and for his guidance and friendship over many years.

都わすれの記

歌祖　文字　撥絃　装釘

谷崎潤一郎　松子

和田三造

四月ある人くゝまく
られて但馬弾を音流

かくあれは桜なかし
つちりや夢の楽る見ふすまし

十五夜

をりひつて
てにほ十五夜
乃月

それそれ
ほうまま
うみの
ちひと
を

みく
弥生を
めよつ
梅の
花

おくれて
ちる
夕づく
夜

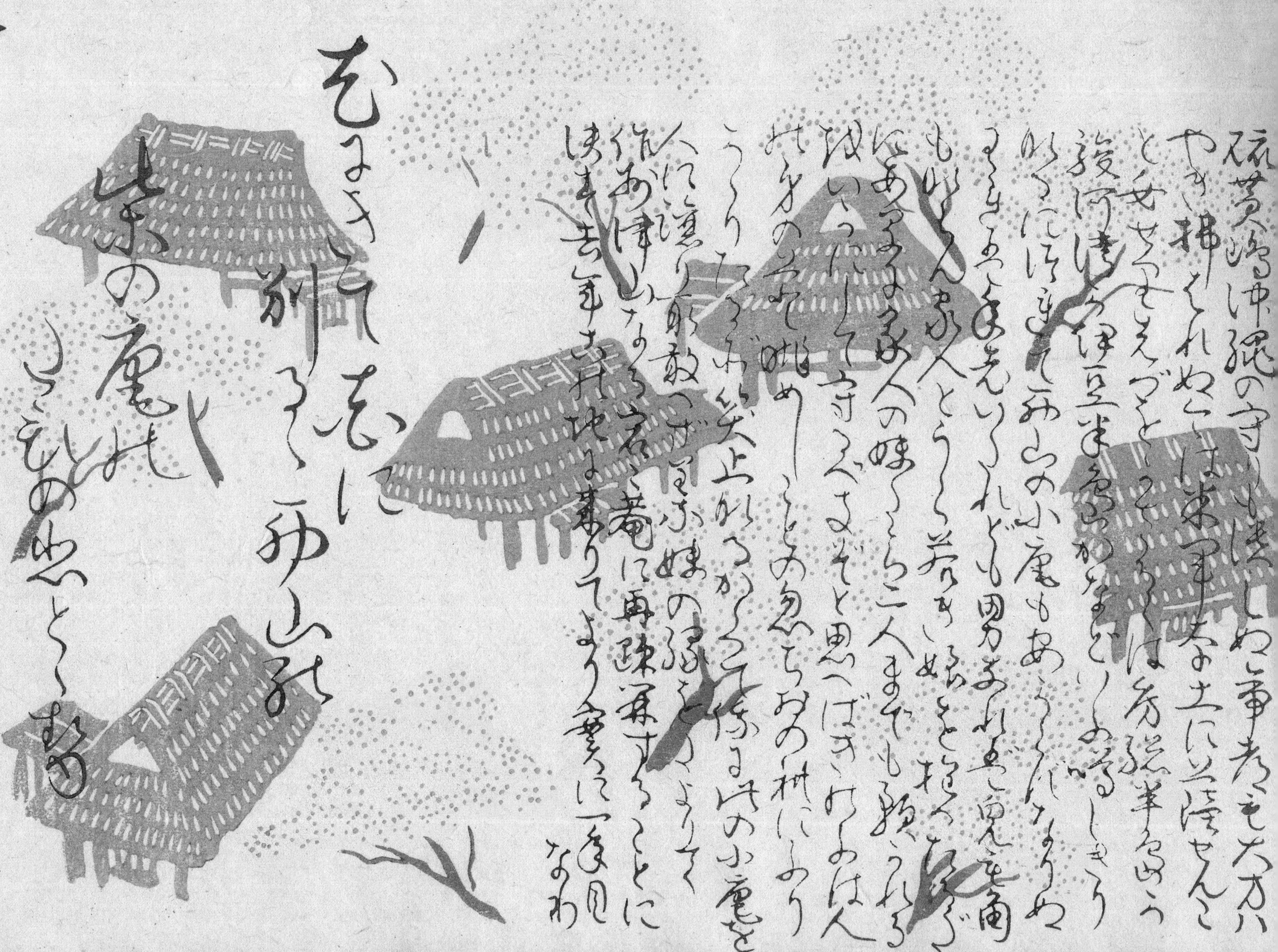

八月七日うちつれて坂神の宮守宅へ音物を奉
りにまうとし まを尽つま来りて 時二月の瑞暁
真棚宮に境矢緑蔭こ三る事にして 今屋廉
棟は御たらうとつよ今はしも待に及
おきほ法の民やそれ候りぬ

煉きぬを
苦しろ
風よろ
れて

つらわに
とつて
おとろうれぬれ

若松振ほまの
庵あうく
うれ

横明つるれ
ふらさその
月

ゆらくの戸ひや
れうやよわつらふ

やきのか
ほまらふ
かろそそて
ある
とらは

戦れをのがれし御れ姫ひも開きし
あとれにすむつ品はたやまく求むつ
さやうもなげ里ぎも接ぼろろを泥
接めくりつはを送うううからうう
糸袖るにのとくに高度の依宿をても
もととをねてる目の里る袖をくこつ
れくくを喰ひ富きねる人をる糸を
しうせととろろ忙しくうううこと
は売りゆくり ことぼ
接こ熱海味本の心をこ
形のらとつのすれし
き松額に屋も
わりふーしや

朝原綻事てめてるくるてや
たこ子れつれも癒をこ
くくし

Memoir of Forgetting the Capital

都わすれの記

（一）

昭和甲申のとしの春、われら一家もまた疎開といふことをせんとて住み馴れし阪神の地を振りすてて行かんとするに、近きあたりの人別れの言葉を求めければ

1. When my family and I also decided to evacuate, in the spring of Showa 19 [1944], and we were about to shake off the earth of our home in Hanshin [the Osaka Kobe region], our neighbors asked for parting words.

あり経なばまたもかへらん津の国の住吉川の松の木かげに
arienaba mata mo kaeran Tsu no kuni no Sumiyoshigawa no matsu no kokage ni

> when time has passed
> we shall come back again!
>> to the shadows of the pines
>> by the Sumiyoshi River
>> in the region of Tsu

（二）

四月十五日、人々に送られて住吉駅を立つ

2. On April 15, seen off by various people, we left Sumiyoshi Station

ふるさとの花に心を残しつつたつや霞の菟原住吉
furusato no hana ni kokoro wo nokoshitsutsu tatsuya kasumi no Ubara Sumiyoshi

> even as my heart remains
> here with the flowers
> of my old home,
>> ah, how the mist is rising
>> as I leave Sumiyoshi in Ubara

（三）

熱海西山の小庵に至れば送り出しし家財道具は早やわれらより先に着きたり、手狭なる家のここかしこに荷を解き物を据ゑなどしてそこはかとなく日を送るほどに、おびただしき山の桜もいつしか盛を過ぎて落花しきり也

3. When we reached the cottage in Nishiyama at Atami, the household goods and furniture we had sent on ahead had arrived before us, and we spent our days distracted, unpacking luggage and putting things in their places in the crowded little house, and before we knew it, days had passed, and the countless cherry blossoms throughout the mountains had all too soon passed their prime, and dropped their petals.

やまざとは桜吹雪に明け暮れて花なき庭も花ぞちりしく
yamazato wa sakura fubuki ni akekurete hana naki niwa mo hana zo chirishiku

day and night swirling
like blowing snow in this mountain
village, these cherry blossoms –
even the garden without
cherry trees   carpeted in blossoms

（四）

家人街にいでて花を購ひ来る、何といふ花ぞと問へばこれなん都わすれといふなりとききて

4. My wife went out to buy flowers. When she asked, "what is this flower called," she was told, "this is the 'forgetting-the-capital' flower."

花の名は都わすれと聞くからに身によそへてぞ佗びしかりける
hana no na wa miyakowasure to kiku kara ni mi ni yosoete zo wabishikarikeru

> as soon as I heard
> the flower's name, forgetting-
> the-capital, this
> aster became part of me,
> and we grieved together!

佗びぬれば都わすれの花にさへおとれる我と思ひけるかな
wabinureba miyakowasure no hana ni sae otoreru ware to omoikeru kana

> grieving I believe
> myself to be even
>   more forlorn
> than the forgetting-
> the-capital flowers

世を佗ぶる山のいほりの床に活けてみやこわすれの花をめでけり
yo wo waburu yama no iori no toko ni ikete miyakowasure no hana wo medekeri

> withdrawn from the world,
> I relish their beauty –
> forgetting-the-capital blossoms,
>   arranged in the alcove
>   of our mountain retreat

19

名にし負はば花よ都は忘るとも世を侘人のわれなわすれそ

な び び と（わびびと）

na ni shi owaba hana yo miyako wa wasuru tomo yo wo wabibito no ware na wasure so

O blossoms! as you bear
it in your name, even as
you forget the capital,
do not forget those like me,
withdrawn from that world

（五）

5.

名にめでて都わすれの花を活けし人ぞみやこを忘れかねたる
na ni medete miyakowasure no hana wo ikeshi hito zo miyako wo wasurekanetaru

     the very one who was
     entranced by their name,
     and arranged the forgetting-
     the-capital flowers, is herself
         unable to forget the capital

（六）
夕ぐれ山に登りて相模湾を望む

6. Climbing up the mountain at dusk, looking out at Sagami Bay

右大臣実朝もまたかくのごと見晴るかしけん沖の初島
udaijin Sanetomo mo mata kaku no goto miharukashiken oki no Hatsushima

     as Sanetomo,
     Minister of the Right, once
     must have done,
     I too look outward to
     Hatsushima, way offshore

（七）
ささやかなる庭の隅に蜜柑の樹あり、六月にもなりぬればその花のにほひ家のうちに薫り来りていにしへの花橘の香もかくやとしのばる

7. In the corner of the little garden there was a *mikan* tree, and when June came, the perfume of its flowers scented the house. I was moved to think that the fragrance from the orange blossoms of ancient times must have been like this.

たそがれに咲ける蜜柑の花一つ老の眼にも見ゆ星の如くに
tasogare ni sakeru mikan no hana hitotsu oi no me ni mo miyu hoshi no gotoku ni

as it blossoms
in the gathering dusk,
to my aging eyes
the single orange blossom
shines forth like a star

（八）
九月某の日、四月ぶりにておのれひとり阪神の旧宅に帰り一ヶ月ほど逗留す、こは神戸青谷にある僅かばかりの土地家屋を抵当に銀行より金を借り出さんがためなり

8. One day in September, I returned alone to our old home in Hanshin after a four-month absence, and stayed for about a month. It was in order to borrow money from the bank using our small house and piece of land in Kobe Aotani as collateral for the loan.

吾妹子をいとしと思へばむらぎものこころをつくし金をつくるも
wagimoko wo itoshi to omoeba muragimo no kokoro wo tsukushi kane wo tsukuru mo

since my beloved
is so dear to me
I am all spent out
    with finding funds
    for us to spend

（九）
故園は荒れてはや昔日の面影はなし

9. My old garden had turned wild, and there was already no trace of its former looks.

すみよしの松のみどりは変らねど頼みし蔭はつゆしげくして
Sumiyoshi no matsu no midori wa kawaranedo tanomishi kage wa tsuyu shigeku shite

the deep green
of the pines of Sumiyoshi
does not change,
but how thick the dew is now
in the shade I so enjoyed

西山の椎の木の間に照る月のかげだにやどれ露の袂に
Nishiyama no shii no ko no ma ni teru tsuki no kage dani yadore tsuyu no tamoto ni

even the moonlight
shining through the oak trees
on the western hills
lingers on my sleeves,
wet with dew

ふるさとの庭に生ひたる蓖麻の実のひまなく妹を恋ひわたるかな
furusato no niwa ni oitaru hima no mi no hima naku imo wo koiwataru kana

if only I could
send my love with
the seeds of this
wonder plant, to the one
who is always on my mind

（十）

今はいづれをかふるさとと云はん、旧宅の庭はいたづらに雑草の生ふるにまかせ防空濠は鼬のすみかとなり果てたるをや

10. Where should I call my old home now? It had come to such a pass that the garden of our old home had been casually left for weeds to grow, and the air raid dugout had become a hangout for weasels.

住み馴れしあとはあれども故郷はあづまになりぬ妹が棲むがに
suminareshi ato wa aredomo furusato wa azuma ni narinu imo ga sumu gani

> traces still remain
> to mark our living here, but
> our real home
> is in the east now –
> where my beloved dwells

ふるさとは今はいづくぞ若草の妻のこもれる伊豆の山家ぞ
furusato wa ima wa izuku zo wakakusa no tsuma no komoreru Izu no yamaga zo

> where is home now?
> the mountain house in Izu
> > the place my wife,
> > sweet as new grass,
> > now lives

24

黒瀬家の令嬢、蘇州領事の許へ嫁ぎ行くとて暇乞ひに見えければ

11. When the young lady of the Kurose family left to marry the consul in Suzhou, she paid us a farewell visit.

古への姑蘇の都の中空にいさよふ月も君を待つらん
inishie no Koso no miyako no nakazora ni isayou tsuki mo kimi wo matsuran

the moon itself
will pause in the firmament
above the ancient
capital of Gusu,
waiting for you

（十二）
十五夜に

12. Fifteenth night

南のはるけき海のたたかひをおもひつつ見る十五夜の月
minnami no harukeki umi no tatakai wo omoitsutsu miru jūgoya no tsuki

while thinking about
the battles raging in the
distant southern seas
I gaze at the full moon
of the fifteenth night

（十三）
十月二日、阪神より入洛して平安神宮に詣る、むかし年々の春毎に家人とその妹たち二人を伴ひて此の神苑の花見に来りしことを思へば感慨禁じ難し

13. When, on October 2, I went from Hanshin into Kyoto to visit the Heian Shrine, I remembered how every spring for years in the past, my wife and her two younger sisters would come to view the blossoms in the shrine garden, and I could not help feeling it deeply.

くれなゐの雨としだれしその春の糸ざくらかや夢のあとかや
kurenai no ame to shidareshi sono haru no itozakura kaya yume no ato kaya

> ah, the weeping cherry
> trees that spring!
> trailing down red
> in the falling rain –
> traces of dreams

雪とばかり袖にちり来し花ならでおつる木の葉ぞ桜なりける
yuki to bakari sode ni chiri koshi hana narade otsuru konoha zo sakura narikeru

> thoughts of snow come
> not from blossom petals
> scattered on my sleeve –
> they are the falling leaves
> from those cherry trees

王城の盛りの春の花さへもかの姉妹にえやはまさりし
ōjō no sakari no haru no hana sae mo kano otodoi ni eya wa masarishi

somehow they surpassed
even the splendor of spring
blossoms at their height
in the capital,
        that bevy of sisters

紅枝垂ゆたにしだるる下蔭をめぐりて立ちし姉と妹
benishidare yutani shidaruru shimokage wo megurite tachishi ane to imōto

beneath the gently
      trailing shadows of the
      weeping red cherries
      they wandered together and
stood there, older and younger sisters

春の日の大極殿の廻廊に立ちつくしけん人々や誰
haru no hi no Daigokuden no kairō ni tachitsukushiken hitobito ya tare

those people spending
the whole springtime day
on the outer corridors
of Daigokuden –
who might they have been?

27

おとどいが袖うちかけし欄干<ruby>欄干<rt>おばしま</rt></ruby>に緋鯉真鯉等けふもつどひ来<ruby>来<rt>く</rt></ruby>
otodoi ga sode uchikakeshi obashima ni higoi magoi ra kyō mo tsudoi ku

      where the sisters' sleeves
      draped over the balustrade,
      today too they have come
      and gather around,
            the red carp and the black carp

春ごとに映りし人の面影を水にとどむと睡蓮の咲く
haru goto ni utsurishi hito no omokage wo mizu ni todomu to suiren no saku

      when, every spring,
      the reflected image
      of my dearest one
      lingers in the pond,
      water lilies start to bloom

春来<ruby>来<rt>く</rt></ruby>ともあやなな咲きそ糸桜見し世の人にめぐり逢ふまで
haru ku tomo ayana na saki so itozakura mishi yo no hito ni meguri au made

      although spring has come
      don't rush to flower,
      o weeping cherry trees!
      until those who have been gone
      come back again

（十四）
大極殿の春の絵葉書に

14. Picture postcard of Daigokuden in spring

糸桜ゆたにしだれて菅の根の長き春日を何ゆめむらん
itozakura yutani shidarete suge no ne no nagaki haruhi wo nani yumemuran

what dreams will gather
around this long spring day
    when the weeping cherry
    trails gently down around
the roots of the graceful sedge

（十五）
十月十日熱海に帰る汽車中

15. October 10, on a train returning to Atami

富士が根は見えそめにけり西山の柴の戸ぼそに立つ顔もみゆ
Fuji ga ne wa miesomenikeri Nishiyama no shiba no toboso ni tatsu kao mo miyu

the base of Mt. Fuji
came into view and I saw too
at Nishiyama
the face of one standing
beside the brushwood gate

（十六）

鹿児島県西南方村泊といふ所の生れなる娘、六年ばかりわが家に奉公して熱海にも附き随ひて来りしが、戦雲漸く南の海に迫ると聞きて親はらからたちの身の上心もとなくや思ひけん、今は暇賜はりて国元へ帰らんといふをいかがはせんとて許しぬ、十一月二十一日来宮駅より立ち行くを見送る人々皆涙を流す、われもまた歌一首よみて贈る

16. Our young woman, who was born in a place called Tomari in Nishi-Minamikata village Kagoshima prefecture, had been in service in our household for about six years, and even accompanied us to Atami. But having heard that the clouds of war were beginning to threaten the southern sea, she had apparently been growing apprehensive about her family's safety, and so she asked if she might be given leave to return home, and we consented. On November 21, all of us who went to see her off at Kinomiya station were in tears, and I offered one poem as well.

さつま潟とまりの浜に漁る日も伊豆のいでゆを忘れざらなん
Satsumagata Tomari no hama ni isaru hi mo Izu no ideyu wo wasurezaranan

even on those days
when you fish on the beach
at Tomari, by the bay of
Satsuma, I am sure you won't forget
the hot springs of Izu

（十七）

年改まりて二月の二十二日雪いたく降りければ

17. After the New Year, on the occasion of a heavy snow on February 22

ふりつもる庭の木の間を眺むれば雪の洞にも隈はありけり
furitsumoru niwa no ko no ma wo nagamureba yuki no hora ni mo kuma wa arikeri

    as I gazed through
        the trees in the garden
where the snow fell in drifts
      in the hollows of the snow
      there were hidden depths

（十八）

そのころ京にも爆弾一つ二つ落ちたりといふ記事新聞に出でしが、やがて吉井勇氏よりおこせる文を見ればいち早く洛東岡崎の家をたたみて富山県八尾町に疎開せりとなり、あまりのことに驚きて返りごとの端に

18. Around that time, the news appeared in newspaper articles that one or two bombs had fallen and destroyed houses even in Kyoto; soon after, Mr. Yoshii Isamu, when he saw the news, packed up his place in Okazaki in eastern Kyoto and evacuated to Yatsuo in Toyama prefecture. I answered his news in the end with great surprise at this turn of events.

ただ頼む越路の山の雪とけてかへる都の春のたよりを
tada tanomu Koshiji no yama no yuki tokete kaeru miyako no haru no tayori wo

    I ask only that
    you send me word
    of spring in Kyoto
      when the snows have melted
      in the Koshiji mountains

おもひやる軒端につもる雪ならで人もわが身もふりまさりゆく
omoiyaru nokiba ni tsumoru yuki narade hito mo waga mi mo furimasariyuku

    it's not the snow
          blanketing the eaves
that moves me so –
it is outdone by the weight
          on my love, on my self

（十九）

なほ此の地のあたたかきにつけてもかの地の寒さいかばかりならん

19. Even though it has warmed up here, how cold it must be there where you are!

みんなみの窓に影さす梅が枝を見つつしおもふ越の白雪
minnami no mado ni kage sasu ume ga e wo mitsutsushi omou Koshi no shirayuki

while I gazed upon
branches of plum trees casting
shadows through the south
facing window, it was on my mind –
the white snow of Koshi

（二十）

20.

吹く風も弥生めきつつ梅の花さくらの如くちる夕かな
fuku kaze mo yayoi mekitsutsu ume no hana sakura no gotoku chiru yūbe kana

the gusting winds
are like the March winds blowing
while the plum tree's
　　　blossoms fall like the cherry –
　　　ah, this is such a night!

（二十一）

硫黄嶋、沖縄の守りも潰えぬ、帝都も大方は焼き払はれぬ、今は米軍本土に上陸せんこと必せり、先づをかさるるは房総半島か、駿河湾か、伊豆半島か、などいふ噂しきりなるにつれて西山の小庵も安からずなりぬ、われは年老いたれども男なれば兎も角もならん、家人とうら若き娘を抱へたるだにあるに家人の妹たち二人までも預かれるをいかにして守るべきぞと思へば、きのふは人の身の上と眺めしことの忽ちおのれにふりかかりたるぞ笑止なる、かくて俄に此の小庵を人に譲り、取敢へず義妹の縁をたよりて作州津山なる宕々庵に再疎開することに決す、去年此の地に来りてより実に一年目なり

21. The defense of both Iwo Jima and Okinawa has collapsed, the Imperial capital is nearly entirely destroyed by fire, and it is now inevitable that the American army will invade the mainland. First of all, as the constant rumors – would it be the Bōsō peninsula, Suruga harbor, the Izu peninsula? – became more insistent, we felt that our little house in Nishiyama was no longer safe. Old though I am, as a man I could probably manage somehow; but on top of having my wife and young daughter to look after, I have been entrusted with my wife's two sisters. What yesterday I thought were other people's troubles suddenly rained down on me, and it was deeply distressing. Somehow, without delay, I had to turn over our place to someone else, and quickly decide to evacuate again. With help from my sister-in-law, we moved to Tōtōan in Tsuyama, Mimasaka. It was actually just one year since we had arrived at this place.

花に来て花に別るる西山の柴の庵の旅のひととせ
hana ni kite hana ni wakaruru Nishiyama no shiba no iori no tabi no hitotose

      having arrived to blossoms
      now I'm parting from blossoms
          at Nishiyama,
      after one full year in a
      wanderer's little brushwood hut

（二十二）

事急なれば此のたびは家財道具など送るべくもあらず、貨車の焼かるることも夥しと聞けばただ日常に欠くべからざ
る品々ばかりをと云ひつつも、いざとなればあれもこれもとて浅ましき数に上りぬ、とかくして五月六日といふに漸
く熱海を発足す

22. Since the situation was urgent, this time we were not able to send all our household goods. We heard that
many freight cars had burned, so we decided to take only those things we needed for everyday use. But even so,
when it came right down to it, with this and that, they piled up, and so we finally departed from Atami on May
sixth.

来宮の 大樟 <ruby>おほくすのき</ruby> の若葉する五月の山をけふぞいでたつ
Kinomiya no ōkusunoki no wakaba suru satsuki no yama wo kyō zo idetatsu

today we leave
these mountains in May
at Kinomiya
where the great camphor trees
are putting forth new leaves

（二十三）

途中阪神の旧宅に立ち寄り数日間休息す、折柄Ｂ二九の群大挙し来り青木深江のあたりなる川西の航空機工場を襲ふ、旧宅より僅か数丁の所なれば天晦く地ふるひ、われら一行と留守番の者共とすべて十四人ささやかなる防空壕に馳せ入りて眼を閉ぢ耳を塞ぐ、實に五月十一日のことなりき

23. On the way, we stopped at our old home in Hanshin to rest for a few days, when a fleet of B29s amassed and struck the Kawanishi airplane factory in the area around Aoki Fukae. When the sky darkened and the earth trembled, since there was a place just a few blocks over from our old home, we all – with the caretakers, a total of fourteen people – rushed into the little air raid shelter, shutting our eyes and covering our ears. This was how we spent May 11th.

かかる世にあふこそ憂けれよき時に我がちちははは失せ給ひけり
kakaru yo ni au koso ukere yoki toki ni waga chichi haha wa usetamaikeri

o grief! to have lived
to meet a world such as this!
I lost them
in good time, my father
and my mother

（二十四）

かくては此処にあらんこと危し、一日も早く作州へ逃れんと家人等の催し立つるままに、五月十四日旧宅を出で、姫路に一泊して翌十五日津山に至る。宕々庵は旧藩主の別業にして池に臨める御殿造りの建物なり

24. This made it clear we were in danger in that place. As the whole household felt impatient to escape to Sakushū as quickly as possible, on May 14 we left our old home, and with a one-night stopover in Himeji, reached Tsuyama the next day, on the fifteenth. Tōtōan was a structure in the palace style, facing a pond, part of a second house of an old feudal lord.

鯉をどり睡蓮しげる水の上にわれも浮身を宿すべきかな
koi odori suiren shigeru mizu no ue ni ware mo ukimi wo yadosu beki kana

the carp are leaping
on the water, the water lilies
flourish, here where
I too must find lodging
for my wandering self

（二十五）
はじめて見る町のすがた趣変りていと珍し、日々吉井川のほとりまでそぞろ歩きす

25. At first sight, the appearance of the town was quite distinctive, really unusual, and every day we strolled along the Yoshii River.

のがれ来てくらすもよしや吉井川河原のほたる橋のゆふかぜ
nogare kite kurasu mo yoshi ya Yoshiigawa kawara no hotaru hashi no yūkaze

> to escape and come here
> to settle was a good thing!
> by the Yoshii River,
> fireflies on the riverbank,
> evening breezes on the bridge

涼みにと川辺へいづる吾妹子に蛍も添うてわたる石橋
suzushimi ni to kawabe e izuru wagimoko ni hotaru mo soute wataru ishibashi

> venturing outside
> to cool off by the riverbank,
> my beloved
> and the fireflies accompanying us
> cross the stone bridge

灯火をいましむる町を小夜ふけてわれは顔にも飛ぶ蛍かな
tomoshibi wo imashimuru machi wo sayo fukete ware wa kao ni mo tobu hotaru kana

> in town where
> streetlights are proscribed
> night falls and fireflies
> flit about our faces –
> masters of the town

（二十六）
近き畑へ菜を乞ひにやるとて

26. Sending someone to beg for greens at a neighboring field

夏の日のあつきめぐみの畑つ物得まくぞほしき豆も玉菜も
natsu no hi no atsuki megumi no hataketsumono emaku zo hoshiki mame mo tamana mo

warmed and blessed
by the hot summer sun,
the fruit of the fields –
what we so longed for!
both the beans and the cabbage

（二十七）
岡山姫路明石などの焼き払はるるに随ひ、此の山間の小都市へも家を失ひ骨肉を失へる人々のさまよひ来る者数を知らず、果ては此の町も何日には焼き払はれんと云ふ風説立ちて、台所道具はもとより畳建具沢庵漬の桶までも車に積みて走り行く者引きもきらざれば、われらもまた一層安全なる地を選ばんには如かじとて、更に西の方十里ばかりなる真庭郡勝山町へ移ることとはなりぬ、一度に多くの乗車券を得ること難ければ、或る日われら夫婦二人、手廻りの荷物五つ六つ持ちて炎天下の津山駅にいたる、その折の悲しさ云はん方なし。

27. As a result of the destruction by fire of Okayama, Himeji, Akashi and other cities, countless numbers of people who had lost their homes and their families came wandering even into this small town folded into the mountains. In the end, there were rumors in the air that this town as well would be firebombed one day. When people were incessantly loading up cars with kitchen goods, not to mention tatami, fixtures, even buckets of pickled radishes, and going off with them, we thought it would be best to choose a safer place to live. It turned out that we could move to the west about 10 ri, to the town of Katsuyama in Maniwa county. It was difficult to obtain many tickets all at once; so one day the two of us, husband and wife, each carrying five or six packages of our belongings, reached Tsuyama station under the blazing sun. The sadness of that occasion is inexpressible.

さすらひの群にまじりて鍋釜を負ひ行く妹をいかにとかせん
sasurai no mure ni majirite nabekama wo oiyuki imo wo ika ni toka sen

indistinguishable in
the vagabond crowd,
moving along with
pots and pans strapped on her back,
what can I do for my beloved?

わらじ売る店屋の軒に家居する燕におとる身にしやはあらぬ
waraji uru miseya no noki ni iei suru tsubame ni otoru mi ni shi ya wa aranu

for someone like me,
lesser than the swallows
living in the eaves
of the store selling straw sandals –
there is nothing I can do

（二十八）

勝山町は旭川の上流なる山峡にありて小京都の名ありといふ、まことは京に比すべくもあらねど山近くして保津川に似たる急流の激するけしき嵐峡あたりの面影なきにしもあらざればしか云ふにや、街にも清き小川ひとすぢ流れたり、われらは休業中の料理屋の離れ座敷一棟を借りて住む、二階の六畳二間を書斎にあてて故辜鴻銘翁が短冊に書したる「有人対月数帰期」の七字を柱に懸けたるは、此の句恰も今のわが身にふさはしければなり、ああわれ齢六十路におよびてかかる辺陬に客とならんとは、げに人の運命ほど測り難きはなし

28. Katsuyama is in a valley at the headwaters of Asahigawa, and is nicknamed "Little Kyoto." Although it really is not to be compared with Kyoto, the mountains are close, and there is some slight resemblance to Arashiyama – in the scenery of the flow of the rapids of the Hozu River; in the town, too, there is the straight clear little river flowing through. We rent and live in a detached building of a closed restaurant. I use two six-mat rooms on the second floor as my study. This verse – written on a *tanzaku* by the late old man Gu Hongming and hanging on a pillar of the study – "someone gazes at the moon, counting the time until returning," is exactly appropriate to my current situation. Ah, when I think that while I am approaching sixty I have come to this, a sojourner in the deep provinces, I realize there is indeed nothing so hard to measure as human fate.

なつかしき都の春の夢さめて空につれなき有明の月
natsukashiki miyako no haru no yume samete sora ni tsurenaki ariake no tsuki

> waking from a dream
> of my longed-for capital
> in the spring,
> > the unfeeling moon
> > in the sky at dawn

まどの戸をあくれば入り来やまざとの人に馴れたる雀うぐひす
mado no to wo akureba iriku yamazato no hito ni naretaru suzume uguisu

> when I open the shutters
> in they come –
> > accustomed to people
> > in the mountain village,
> > the swallow, the warbler

（二十九）

或る夜川のほとりに笛を曳きしに、思ひもかけずうるはしき洋琴のおと聞え来りて橋の欄干にもたれつつ恍惚となりぬ、そは横浜より疎開し来りし令嬢のつれづれにまかせて奏るなり、その洋琴もその人のはるばる運ばせ来しものぞと教へられて、その後漸くたよりを求め、家人等をいざなひてかの麗人の僑居にいたり改めて数曲を所望したりけり

29. One evening as we walked by the river, we unexpectedly heard the lovely sound of a piano, and we leaned against the balustrade of the bridge, enraptured. We had been told that the piano had been moved the whole distance when the family evacuated from Yokohama, and was played in her leisure by the young lady of the household.   We finally were introduced after that, and our whole family was invited to hear several pieces played by the young beauty in her temporary dwelling.

佗人は涙ぞすなる久方の月の都の糸竹のこゑ

wabibito wa namida zo su naru hisakata no tsuki no miyako no itotake no koe

how our tears flow,
we exiles here, at the voice
of music as if from
the capital itself, beneath
the far distant palace of the moon

（三十）

八月七日、かねて阪神の留守宅へ荷物を取りに遣はしし者共戻り来りて昨六日の払暁応接間に焼夷弾落下、三分間にして全屋灰燼に帰したりといふ、今はわれらも帰るに家なき流浪の民とはなりぬ

30. On August 7, people whom we had sent to bring back some belongings from our empty house in Hanshin told us that at daybreak on the previous day, August 6, an incindiary bomb was dropped and fell in the front parlor, and in three minutes the entire house was reduced to ashes. Now even should we return, we too have become wanderers without a home.

秋来ぬと告ぐる風より故郷のたよりに先づぞおどろかれぬる
aki kinu to tsuguru kaze yori furusato no tayori ni mazu zo odorokarenuru

more surprising than the word
the wind brings
that autumn has come
is the shock of the news
of our old home lost

草枕旅寝の床にしのぶかな焼野が原のふるさとの月
kusamakura tabine no toko ni shinobu kana yakeno ga hara no furusato no tsuki

in my wanderer's bed,
grass for my pillow,
I call it to mind –
the moon of my old home shines
on an expanse of burned fields

故郷はやけのが原となりはててゆふべの露やおきぞわづらふ
furusato wa yakeno ga hara to narihatete yūbe no tsuyu ya oki zo wazurau

my old home has
ended as an expanse of
burned fields,
and the embers
distress the evening dew

（三十一）
東京の街も殆ど何物も残らずと聞きて

31. On hearing that nearly nothing is left of the streets of Tokyo.

むさし野は草よりいでて草に入る月の都となりやしぬらん
musashino wa kusa yori idete kusa ni iru tsuki no miyako to nari ya shinuran

> Musashino has
> become the capital of
> > the moon rising from
> > the grasses and returning
> to fade into the grasses

（三十二）
八月十五日終戦

32. August 15; war over

思ひやれつはものどもが剣太刀すてしゆふべの野辺の露けさ
omoiyare tsuwamonodomo ga tsurugi tachi suteshi yūbe no nobe no tsuyu kesa

> only think of it!
> all the nation's warriors
> have discarded their
> long swords   last night's fields
> > heavy with dew, with tears

（三十三）
敗戦の秋やうやくたけなはにして家なき身のあはれさはひとしほなり

33. After the defeat at long last, at the height of autumn homeless people were all the more filled with pathos.

荻の葉のゆふべの露もおもひやれことしは袖の秋の深さを
ogi no ha no yūbe no tsuyu mo omoiyare kotoshi wa sode no aki no fukasa wo

    evening dew
    on the plume grass
    feels it too
        this year
    the depth of autumn on my sleeve

たたかひにやぶれし国の秋深み野にも山にもなく虫の声
tatakai ni yabureshi kuni no aki fukami no ni mo yama ni mo naku mushi no koe

    in a country
        defeated in battle
        the depths of autumn:
    from the fields, from the mountains,
    voices of insects calling

（三十四）
長雨ふりつづきて旭川をはじめ所々の河川あふれ橋あまた流れしかど人手も資材も使ひつくせる後のことなれば多くはそのままに捨て置かれたり

34. Heavy rains continued, and the Asahi River and other rivers overflowed. Many bridges were swept away; and even after using the efforts of many people and many materials, most were abandoned.

大水のあとに残りし橋げたのなほ日毎にもくづれゆくかな
ōmizu no ato ni nokorishi hashigeta no nao higoto ni mo kuzureyuku kana

in the aftermath
of the flood, the girders
                    of the bridge are left
day after day
to fall to pieces

（三十五）
されどもたまたま美しき秋日和もなきにあらず

35. However, it isn't that we didn't have beautiful clear fall weather every now and then.

老いぬれば事ぞともなき秋晴れの日の暮れゆくもをしまれにけり
oi nureba koto zo tomonaki akibare no hi no kureyuku mo oshimarenikeri

> it comes with getting
> old! I find myself
> regretting
> the unavoidable passing
> of a bright autumn day

（三十六）
或る夜

36. One night

星冴ゆる空と見えつつ小夜ふけてふとおどろかす村しぐれ哉
hoshi sayuru sora to mietsutsu sayo fukete futo odorokasu murashigure kana

> as I gazed up
> at a sky rich with stars
> night deepened –
> the sudden surprise of
> heavy autumn showers

（三十七）
冬来る

37. Winter comes

柿の実の熟れたる汁にぬれそぼつ指つめたく冬は来にけり
kaki no mi no uretaru shiru ni nuresobotsu oyobi tsumetaku fuyu wa kinikeri

my fingers, drenched
in the juice of a ripe
persimmon,
are chilled –
winter has come

すさまじとかねても聞きし山里の物みな凍る冬は来にけり
susamaji to kanete mo kikishi yamazato no mono mina ko'oru fuyu wa kinikeri

I've already heard
how dreadful it is – winter,
when everything
in this mountain village
freezes – winter has come

（三十八）
師走二十九日同じ町のうちなる旅館の二階に移りて越年す

38. On Dec. 29, we moved in the same village to the second floor of an inn and saw out the old year.

美作の山のかひなる旅籠屋に春を迎ふるとしもありけり
Mimasaka no yama no kai naru hatagoya ni haru wo mukauru toshi mo arikeri

this was the year
we greeted the spring
　　　from an inn
in a gorge in the mountains
of Mimasaka

（三十九）
雪の歌数首

39. Several poems on snow

はるけくも北に海ある国に来て南になりぬ雪のやまやま
harukeku mo kita ni umi aru kuni ni kite minami ni narinu yuki no yamayama

    we have come so far
        to a country with the sea
            to the north
  and now the snow-covered mountains
          lie to our south

雪ふかき軒のつららのつらつらに都こひしき日を送るかな
yuki fukaki noki no tsurara no tsuratsura ni miyako koishiki hi wo okuru kana

    icicles hanging
    from snow-laden eaves–
    I pass the days
    in great longing
    for the city of Kyoto

いとほしや雪のふる日の城山を都の山に似たりといふ人
ito'oshi ya yuki no furu hi no Shiroyama wo miyako no yama ni nitari to iu hito

    how unsettling!
    to hear her compare
    Shiroyama on a snowy day
    to the mountains
    encircling Kyoto

しめやかに団欒しをればさやさやと障子にきゆるうすゆきのおと

shimeyaka ni madoishi oreba sayasaya to shōji ni kiyuru usuyuki no oto

sitting quietly together,
the sound of rustling,
as the light snow
hits and disappears against
the sliding paper doors

（四十）
渡辺夫人に

40. To Mrs. Watanabe

おりたちて馴れぬ厨の水仕事したまふ人に白雪のふる
oritachite narenu kuriya no mizushigoto shitamau hito ni shirayuki no furu

white snow falls
on one who resolutely
does for us the service
of kitchen chores
she'd never done before

（四十一）
春来る

41. Spring comes

山里に春は来ぬらし門に出て縄跳びすなり二十乙女も
yamazato ni haru wa kinu rashi kado ni dete nawatobi su nari hatachi otome mo

   it seems that spring
   has come at last to this
   mountain village:

   when I step from my gate,
   a twenty-year-old girl is jumping rope

漸くに雪は晴れたりうなゐらはつららを折りてもてあそぶなり
yōyaku ni yuki wa haretari unaira wa tsurara wo orite moteasobu nari

   at long last
   the snow has cleared
   the little boys
   break off icicles
   to play around

あまさかる鄙のなまりを聞きわびし耳にさやけき鶯のこゑ
amasakaru hina no namari wo kiki wabishi mimi ni sayakeki uguisu no koe

   growing weary of
   hearing the accents
   of this distant countryside,
     the voice of the warbler
     is bright to my ear

（四十二）
いつまでかく山籠りしてあらんもあぢきなし、今は都近きあたりに住むべき家を求めばやとて、弥生のなかば過ぎ、屈強の男に米醤油など背負はせて先づ己れひとり京に上る

42. Wondering how long we would remain shut away in the mountains, and thinking that now would be a good time to look for a house to live in near Kyoto, shortly after mid-March I had a strong, wiry fellow carry some rice and soy sauce on his back for me, and went ahead by myself to the capital.

たたかひに破れし国も春なれや四条五条の人のゆきかひ
tatakai ni yabureshi kuni mo haru nare ya Shijō Gojō no hito no yukikai

> even to a country
> defeated in battle
> spring has come!
> people coming and going
> on Fourth Avenue, Fifth Avenue

京極のちまたの塵もなつかしやむかしながらの都と思へば
Kyōgoku no chimata no chiri mo natsukashi ya mukashi nagara no miyako to omoeba

> even the dust
> in the streets of Kyōgoku
> makes me nostalgic!
> when I think how the capital
> is just as it was in the past

国は破れ人はすさみし春ながら都は嵯峨の花ざかりかな
kuni wa yabure hito wa susamishi haru nagara miyako wa Saga no hana zakari kana

> the nation defeated,
> the people grown rough –
>   even so it is spring –
> the capital, with
> Saga in full bloom

（四十三）

戦禍をのがれし街の賑ひは聞きしにまされど住むべき家はたやすく求むべきやうもなければ、旅館貸間などを経めぐりつつ日を送るうち、からくも上京鞍馬口の近くに当座の仮寓を定むることを得て五月の末に待ちこがれし人々を呼び寄せぬ、家人は京に来しうれしさはさることながら、ことしの花におくれしことを悔み、熱海以来の心労に身のおとろへの著しきを歎じけるもわりなしや

43. The bustle in the streets, which had escaped the ravages of war, was even greater than I had heard, but the search for a house to live in was not at all easy. While I paid for lodging, days passed as I searched around with difficulty, until finally I was able to settle on a temporary residence in upper Kyoto near Kurama-guchi.   In late May I called my long-waiting family to come join me. While I was inexpressibly glad when my wife reached Kyoto, still she regretted she was too late for the cherry blossoms, and I could not but mourn, though it does no good, the great toll on her that the hardships she has suffered since leaving Atami have taken.

朝寝髪枕きてめでにしいくとせの手馴れの顔も痩せにけらしな
asanegami makite medenishi ikutose no tanare no kao mo yasenikerashi na

> stroking your
> tousled hair, beloved,
>   for so many years
>   familiar to my touch,
> how thin your face has grown

Memoir of Forgetting the Capital
都 わ す れ の 記

2010 年 11 月 2 日発行

著　　者	谷 崎 潤 一 郎
訳　　者	エミー・ハインリック
序　　文	ド ナ ル ド・キ ー ン
口　　絵	（文字）谷 崎 松 子
	（挿絵）和 田 三 造
発 行 者	新 田 満 夫
発 行 所	株式会社 雄 松 堂 書 店

〒 160-0002
東京都新宿区坂町 27
電話　03-3357-1449（編集）
　　　03-3357-1446（営業）

印刷・製本　ミズノプリテック株式会社
ISBN 978-4-8419-0547-2